White Monkey King

A CHINESE FABLE

Retold by Sally Hovey Wriggins

Illustrated by Ronni Solbert

PANTHEON BOOKS

For Anne Swann Goodrich who introduced me to
Wu Ch'êng-ên, and with gratitude to Elizabeth
Benson Booz.

Text Copyright © 1977 by Sally Hovey Wriggins
Illustrations © 1977 by Ronni Solbert
All rights reserved under International and Pan-American
Copyright Conventions. Published in the United States by
Pantheon Books, a division of Random House, Inc., and
simultaneously in Canada by Random House of Canada Limited,
Toronto. Manufactured in the United States of America.

Library of Congress Cataloging in Publication Data

Wriggins, Sally Hovey.   White Monkey King.
Adaptation of the first part of Hsi yu chi by Ch'êng-ên Wu.
SUMMARY: A mischievous monkey acquires god-like powers
and creates havoc in heaven. First part of a translation
of the Chinese legend as retold in the
sixteenth-century novel "Journey to the West."
1. Monkeys—Legends and stories. [1.
Folklore—China.
2. Monkeys—Fiction] I. Solbert, Ronni.
II. Wu, Ch'êng-ên, ca. 1500–ca. 1582. Hsi yu chi. III. Title.
PZ8.1.W88Wh   813".5"4   [398.2]   76–44281
ISBN 0–394–83450–X   ISBN 0–394–93450–4 lib. bdg.
0 9 8 7 6 5 4 3 2 1

Contents

Introduction

There once was a monk who traveled four thousand miles across the Gobi Desert and over three ranges of some of the highest mountains in the world on his way from China to India. He did it in the seventh century, and his pilgrimage became one of the great legends of China. In the sixteenth century a man named Wu Ch'êng-ên wove these legends into a long novel, which he called *Journey to the West*. In this famous story, part myth, part fantasy, the monk is accompanied on his journey by a monkey.

In *White Monkey King,* I have retold only

the first part of the story, in which the mischievous monkey acquires god-like powers and creates havoc in heaven. A sequel, *Monkey King Goes West,* will describe the journey of monk and monkey to India.

There are several translators of *Journey to the West*—Arthur Waley, Dr. Anthony C. Yu, and George Theiner. For my retelling I worked with Sylvia Lo Dudbridge. She translated for me from the original Chinese the first part of what has come to be known in English as the Monkey Story. The pleasures of retelling as well as responsibility for the final version rest, however, with the author. I am indebted to both Sylvia and her husband, Dr. Glenn Dudbridge of Oxford University, for their interest and scholarship.

White Monkey King

1

The Intruder

White Monkey grabbed a fat vine hanging
down from a camphor tree and swung with it
over the Fan Shi River. He landed on the other
side in a tree full of brown monkeys. What a
face he had—an intelligent brow, blazing eyes,
and a nose twitching for mischief.

"I remember when I was born," he exclaimed as he dropped to the ground.

Two brown monkeys followed him. "What
did he say?" asked a bearded, wise monkey.

"I didn't hear it," a large and lazy monkey
said.

White Monkey's eyes flashed. His body, as

silver-white as the moon, hummed with the secret of it. "I remember when I was born on the Mountain of Flowers and Fruit," he repeated loudly.

The two brown monkeys snickered. The rest of the monkeys swung down around them and began swatting one another.

"First I was a stone monkey."

They stopped swatting. "A stone monkey?" they said, scratching their ears.

"Then one day I felt something warm on my back. It got hotter and hotter. There was a melting feeling right here," he said, pointing to his chest. "The melting feeling oozed out to my paws and to the tip of my tail."

"Didn't it hurt?" the brown monkeys cried.

"No. I just felt warm and tingly, and my toes twitched. Suddenly I could move. I shook each leg, hopped up and down, and leaped up to a branch like that one there."

Their eyes followed his silvery body as he sprang onto a shaggy limb above them.

"I was born of the union of Heaven and Earth," White Monkey said to himself as he looked up at the sky. "But that is too great a mystery for simple telling."

All the brown monkeys on the ground blinked in the hot morning sun and began shaking their heads and pulling on the the tips of their ears. Surely he was joking. Monkeys never remembered when they were born. They left him to his perch and sought the shade of a familiar mulberry tree whose branches were so wide that they could shelter a hundred monkeys. Lolling in its comfortable limbs, they closed their eyes and sniffed the sweet-scented ferns below as if they wished to forget the intruder.

White Monkey interrupted them. "Let's follow the river. I'll bet there is a secret spring up on that mountain."

The river running past them flowed green in its wide, deep channel. Farther up the mountainside the water foamed white as it tumbled over dark rocks, splashing and laughing its way down the valley.

"Come on," White Monkey shouted. "Let's see if we can find where the river begins. The water there will be very sweet."

Was there really a beginning? What was sweet water? The brown monkeys had never thought about such things before. They dropped down from their mulberry tree, a few at first and then more and more of them. Finally all of them bounded up the mountainside, leaping from boulder to boulder. What was the river's secret? They ran to find out. After a while, they forgot why they were running and began trudging along bowlegged, on all fours, dragging their toes. Oh, but were they tired.

Gradually the water music changed—the first soft drumming sound grew louder. The monkeys looked up. Eighty or ninety feet above them a white form moved across the dark boulders.

"It's a white tiger," one monkey screamed.

"No, it's a panther. Let's go back!"

"Don't be foolish," Wise Monkey shouted. "It's White Monkey."

Higher on the mountain they caught up with White Monkey, not far from a place where a light mist hovered over the river. There was a rainbow inside the mist. Hooting with delight, they raced up to have a closer look. Behind the mist flowed a shining silver water curtain. All the monkeys gasped as they lined up in front of it. Lazy Monkey chuckled to himself, not a very

nice chuckle, and strode over to White Monkey.

"If you're so eager to explore the river, why don't you jump through the water curtain?"

"Yes, yes," cried all the monkeys. "Tell us what's on the other side."

"If you come back, then you can be our king," Wise Monkey said, but with doubting eyes, as if he thought White Monkey probably wouldn't return.

White Monkey didn't like water, but he did like taking a dare. He braced himself, took one flying leap, and went straight through the water curtain. When he opened his eyes again, he was standing on dry land. Before him arched a shining bridge. He ran up to the hump of the bridge and stopped. A mysterious grotto, whose walls were blue and green like an exotic shell, shone in the afternoon sunlight. He glanced at the words carved on the rock above the cave. In front of the cave he saw almond trees and peach trees around a grassy place filled with stone chairs and stone tables laden with stone cups and plates. There was even a large stone boat for the monkeys to play in.

"How splendid! What a perfect find!" He

could hardly wait to tell the other monkeys. He ran down the bridge, braced himself, took one great leap through the waterfall, and landed on the other side near Wise Monkey.

"What was it like?" Wise Monkey asked.

Lazy Monkey elbowed his way through the crowd. "Was there lots of water?" he said in a loud voice, pushing two monkeys aside.

White Monkey jumped to the highest rock above them to escape the screaming and shoving.

"Tell us, tell us," they pleaded. "Tell us what was there."

"It is a miracle," he replied and described the bridge, the cave, the peach trees, and the stone tables and chairs. "It is called the Cave of the Water Curtain on the Mountain of Flowers and Fruit in the land of Ao Lai*."

"How do you know?" asked a little monkey.

"There's an inscription carved over the opening of the cave. Come on, I'll show you."

At first they all stood back, rubbing their chests, tugging at each other's ears, and scratching one another's backs. Then they

---

*China

pretended to be gazing at far-off places or thinking deep thoughts. How could they possibly jump through the water curtain when they were so busy?

"Here, take my arm," White Monkey said to Wise Monkey. "And you," pointing to Lazy Monkey. "It was your idea. Take my other arm. Come on."

The three of them crouched down, closed their eyes, and took a flying leap through the water curtain. The other monkeys grew wobbly in the knees and chattered with fear. Finally one of the big monkeys jumped too, and the little ones gave shrieks of fright and delight. A small monkey did it, and then the mother monkeys with babies on their backs did it. Next came the scrawny monkeys and frightened monkeys. In the end, everyone jumped through.

"I wasn't scared," they all said to one another on the other side.

"Weren't you scared?"

"No, of course not."

"Oh, I'll bet you were. I saw your knees shaking."

This talk got tiresome, so they popped off in

all directions like a string of firecrackers. They scarcely saw the cave with the blue-green walls, they were so busy tossing stone cups in the air and upsetting all the tables. They dragged the stone chairs around, had a peach fight, and began squabbling over the best place to sit in the stone boat. White Monkey waited for them to exhaust themselves. Then he stood on the shining bridge to address them.

"Monkeys," he shouted, "you promised that if I jumped through the water curtain I could be your king. I have gone through it three times. I have also found you a fine place to live. It is big enough for hundreds of us here by the bridge, and we have hardly begun to explore the mountain."

Loud cries of enthusiasm filled the air. "Great King, long live the King!" A few peaches were tossed around in all the excitement. White Monkey King snarled and the throwing stopped. He announced that there would be a grand celebration that very evening. Now monkeys love nothing better than eating and having parties, so all afternoon they scoured their mountain for its flowers and fruit.

"Fling garlands of wisteria from the trees,"

Monkey King commanded when the monkeys returned with huge glowing bunches of peaches, plums, and red cherries. Lazy Monkey supervised the making of wine. At last all was ready. Monkey King sat at the head of the longest table. "Here's to each and every monkey in my kingdom," he shouted, raising his cup to salute his subjects. Everyone toasted everyone else. Monkey King announced that Wise Monkey would be his chief minister and that Lazy Monkey would be his first lieutenant. This brought great applause and more speeches. In the end, everyone stood on the tables shouting, "Great King! Long life, King Monkey! Great King! One thousand years!"

Monkey King's eyes flashed. His body hummed. "A long life together, my monkeys," he answered, without realizing what was to come.

2

The Search

For twenty-five years Monkey King inspired his subjects, until his kingdom was the greatest in the northern world. Everyone was content except, oddly enough, Monkey King himself. His many achievements, his power, and the devotion of his subjects no longer satisfied him. The fire in his eyes seemed to go out. After meeting with his ministers, Wise Monkey and Lazy Monkey, he used to lock himself up in his peach courtyard. There he was so often lost in gloomy thoughts, that his ministers grew alarmed.

Monkey King had one favorite peach tree,

which stood, flowerless, in the middle of his courtyard. He feared that it was dying. One day a flock of green birds alighted on its bare branches and Monkey King knew that this was a good omen. His tree would bloom again.

The following night he had a strange dream, so strange that he called his trusted ministers to his bedside. "I dreamed," Monkey King said, "of a mountain that glows at night. But that's not all. In the daytime this mountain seemed to have crystal blue air around it. Well, I thought in my dream that I would like to climb that mountain."

Wise Monkey nodded his head sadly as if he already knew what was going to happen.

"Then I saw men with crowns of light going over the peak. Who were they?" Monkey King demanded. "Where do they live?"

"There are such men in ancient caves on sacred mountains," replied Wise Monkey. "They live beyond the sea in faraway lands. My great-grandfather visited them years and years ago."

"How can I find them?" Monkey King asked, his eyes blazing again. "Who are these men?"

"Buddhas, Immortals, and Sages," Wise Monkey answered.

"I must go and see them," Monkey King said. "You, Wise Monkey, shall rule in my absence."

Wise Monkey bowed.

Lazy Monkey shook his head. "Why go all that way to see a Buddha or whatever they are?"

"You wouldn't understand." Monkey King replied. He turned to Wise Monkey and said, "I will leave in a few days on my journey. See that the necessary preparations are made."

Lazy Monkey persisted. "But why go so far to see Buddhas and Immortals? Aren't we enough for you?"

"Of course you are," Monkey King said, getting up. "It's only that I should like to have a crown of light around my head, too." He flipped his tail. "Just the thing for a monkey king."

So it was that Monkey King prepared to depart. In a very few days all was ready, and he pushed off on a raft heaped with peaches and plums, bags of nuts, and all kinds of life-giving herbs. He floated down to sea on the Fan Shi

River. A strong wind sent him flying over the Southern Sea, to a strange continent where he trudged through little fishing villages and lands with wild forests, looking for someone with a crown of light. Then one day, on the crest of a hill, he caught sight of another wide blue ocean. He rolled all the way down the slope and turned twenty-five somersaults at the bottom.

Monkey King made another raft like the first one and loaded it down with piles of fruit and nuts. How long this second ocean trip lasted, Monkey King couldn't tell. Months of sailing seemed like a year. He missed his monkeys and the Water Curtain Cave. After a time, the air grew clearer as though each particle had been bathed by the sun. A white heron flew overhead. Monkey King knew that land was not far off.

As he neared the shore, he saw the crystal blue mountain of his dream in the distance. Monkey King couldn't believe it. He sailed in, beached his raft, and began hiking toward the mountain. As he climbed higher the air seemed to dance with blue crystals. A dark forest loomed before him. He ran toward it and was swinging through the trees when he heard a woodsman singing about an Immortal named Subhuti, who lived at the Cave of the Crescent Moon and Three Stars.

Monkey King followed the woodsman's directions to the cave, tramping along for several hours, until he came to a reddish cliff overlooking a stream. A cave full of terraces and little balconies had been cut out of the red rock. At the right side was an inscription—Cave of the Crescent Moon and Three Stars. He banged at the entrance door. No one answered. That was strange. Monkey King leaped up to the branches of a tall pine tree to look around. He stuffed himself with pine seeds and was just about to see if he could bounce them off the door when a young boy came out.

Monkey King dropped to the ground. "Don't tell me I came all this way just to see you?"

"And who may you be, wild animal?" asked the boy.

"I am White Monkey King from the Mountain of Flowers and Fruit in the land of Ao Lai," Monkey King said, bowing low.

"What is your wish?"

"I'm searching for an Immortal, but that's

probably beyond you, for I see you've hardly lost your baby teeth."

"My teacher is wise and seeks the Truth," the boy said.

"Well then, show me in, for I have come a long way," Monkey King said, flipping his tail.

The boy opened the door onto the dim light of a cool, dark vault. Monkey King followed him through a long corridor with rooms on either side to a grand assembly hall. At the far side of this hall, a yellow-robed monk sat on a jade platform. A cluster of young monks and students were sitting cross-legged on the floor at his feet. Monkey King walked to the platform and bowed low. When he looked up, he saw a face full of light, the radiance of the great teacher Subhuti.

"Master, as pupil to teacher, I kneel before you."

"And where may you be from?" asked the wise old one.

"I come from the Mountain of Flowers and Fruit in the land of Ao Lai," Monkey King replied, bowing low once again.

"That cannot be. China is too far away. There are two seas and the entire southern

continent between us. Besides, I know the people of China. They are a foxy, untrustworthy lot."

"Reverend Master, I assure you," Monkey King said, bowing yet again. "I have been journeying for three years. Truly I have wandered far and have sailed over two oceans."

"Very well," Subhuti replied. "I believe you. And where is your family from?"

"I have no family."

"Who may your parents be then?" Subhuti asked.

"I have no parents either."

"Pray, how is that?"

"I remember when I was born. I grew from a magic stone on the Mountain of Flowers and Fruit," Monkey King replied.

Subhuti thought to himself, "*That is impossible for ordinary creatures. It must mean that he is born of the union of Heaven and Earth. If he passes all my tests, he has the potential for god-like powers.*"

Subhuti gave Monkey King a religious name made up of long words the monkey didn't understand and said that he would accept him as a pupil.

For the next few months Monkey King burned incense, worked in the bamboo grove, and performed his daily chores. A fat monk brought rice for his evening meal and slipped him fresh peaches and bananas. His studies began, and they were very puzzling. He realized that it would take many years to begin to understand even a little of Subhuti's teachings. However, the years did pass, and Monkey King made great progress.

One day the Master agreed to talk about the Great Way, the true path. All his students seated themselves in the large assembly hall. Monkey King was so enchanted by Subhuti's words that his mouth was full of laughter. He couldn't stop drumming his feet, scratching his ears, and making music with his tail. He was just about to turn a cartwheel when the Master caught sight of him.

"What is the matter with you that you are so jumpy and cannot be still?" Subhuti asked.

"Oh, but I love what you say. If I seem to jiggle about, it is only because I am listening with my whole self and taking it all in," Monkey King replied.

"Ah, so you understand the subtle meaning

of my lecture?" the Master said. "Pray, how long have you been here?"

"I guess it must be five years now," replied Monkey King, swinging his arms up and down.

"What kind of wisdom do you seek?" Subhuti asked.

"I'm not sure. What about learning how to be either a Buddha, an Immortal, or a Sage?"

"Do you know what these beings are?"

"No, but I am all ears." Monkey King cupped his ears with his hands. "See?"

"A Sage is wise because he learns much from reading—"

"I'm not so good at reading. That's not for me," Monkey King cut in. "What about becoming a Buddha?"

"A Buddha lives so he has right desires."

"What does that mean?" Monkey King asked, hopping up and down.

"He has taught himself to want only what is good."

"That's definitely not for me," Monkey King said. "Tell me about Immortals."

"An Immortal is one who lives forever," Subhuti replied.

"I'd like that," Monkey King said, swinging his tail. "I don't particularly want to die, and I wouldn't mind living forever."

"But you would have to learn to sit still."

Monkey King let his tail slap the floor. "Maybe that is not for me either."

"You miserable creature," Subhuti said. "You don't like anything."

"Wait a minute. I like to conquer things. I do it all the time," Monkey King said.

Subhuti stepped off the jade platform and came up to Monkey King. He struck him three times on the head with a stick, folded his hands behind his back, stalked out of the room to his private chamber, and slammed the door behind him.

All the other pupils were furious. "You ruined everything. Why couldn't you sit quietly and listen like everyone else? Don't you see how you've insulted him? The Master was going to tell us about the secret of the golden flower, and now he's so angry that he never will."

Monkey King took their abuse without answering back. The fact of the matter was, that he understood Subhuti's hidden message. By hitting him three times, the Master meant that he should come at the third watch of the night. By folding his hands behind him, the Master intended for him to enter through the back door. By slamming the door, Subhuti meant for him to enter the inner chamber so that he could be taught the Truth in secrecy.

Monkey King could hardly wait. What would the Master tell him? The rest of the day seemed endless, and when Monkey King finally went to his sleeping mat he could not, dared not, go to sleep.

3

The Instruction in Magic

His small face peeked out from behind his paws for a minute. A splash of white from the moon was shining in his eyes. He covered his eyes again and started to count the minutes and hours. Monkey King counted five hundred breaths and crooked up one finger. He meant to crook up two fingers when he reached one thousand breaths, but he was so excited that he got mixed up.

His audience with Subhuti was to be at the third watch. Surely it must be almost time. He couldn't stand waiting anymore. He got up and tiptoed out of his room. Everyone else was asleep in the little rooms off the assembly hall. There was no sound, not even the hoot of an owl. Monkey King crept down a corridor lined with tiny, flickering oil lamps until he came to the Master's chamber. The door was half open. He went in and knelt down by the bed. Sandalwood incense filled the air and made him think of cinnamon sticks. Subhuti's face was turned toward the wall. What should Monkey King do?

"It's so difficult, so very difficult," Subhuti murmured. "The Way is most secret. The Truth must be guarded carefully."

Monkey cleared his throat.

Subhuti sat up with a start. "And what may you be doing here, jumpy Monkey?"

"It's the third watch, Reverend Master," Monkey began. "I have come by the back gate to receive private instruction. Just as you told me by your secret signs."

"Oh yes," Subhuti nodded.

Monkey King sniffed. He liked the smell of sandalwood.

"I see you are truly hungry for secret knowledge," Subhuti said, sitting squarely on his mat and crossing his legs in the lotus position.

Monkey King nodded. He watched the inner light of Subhuti glow in the darkness.

"Since yours is a special destiny," Subhuti said, "I shall reveal to you the sacred formula of long life. The illustrious Lao Tzu first discovered it and taught it to my teacher who taught it to me. Are you ready?"

Monkey King closed his eyes.

Subhuti recited the sacred formula.

Monkey King kept his eyes shut until he had learned it by heart. When he opened them, his eyes had a faraway look, as if he had just awakened from a long sleep. He trembled and shook himself. Monkey King never knew how he found his way back to his room.

For a long time Monkey King was content to follow the rules of his teacher. He pondered. He studied. He meditated. He did his chores, avoiding mischief in every form. A year later Subhuti told him that the time had come for him to learn how to change from one form to another.

"You must learn to transform your size, your shape, and your color just as a magician does. Come closer, and listen to what I have to say." Subhuti sat down under an ancient plum tree

crossing his legs in the lotus position. Monkey King sat at his feet and closed his eyes.

He peeked with one eye and shut it quickly.

Silence.

Monkey looked again and saw the light around Subhuti growing brighter. Gradually the stillness unfolded like a flower.

Subhuti recited the magic formulas for transforming himself. He gave instruction as to how each kind of change should be carried out and warned Monkey King to protect his lute bone. If this bone in his chest were ever injured, he would never again be able to transform himself. They sat together for a long time. Under the Master's guidance Monkey King actually turned himself into a buzzard and then a small pine tree. Subhuti was pleased with his progress.

Several months later Subhuti taught him a fixing magic so that he could make someone as still as a statue. Another time he showed him a multiplying trick. Monkey King had to pull a few hairs from his body, bite them into pieces, and call "transform". At once, hundreds of tiny white monkeys would appear. They would follow his commands until he shouted "trans-

form" again, and then they would disappear, becoming nothing more than white hairs again.

"Oh my," he said to himself, "the possibilities are boundless. Boundless."

"Now Monkey," Subhuti cautioned him. "I have taught you these skills over a long period of time and watched you closely. You must use these gifts wisely. They are not for playing."

Monkey King's final lesson came when he was preening himself on top of Holy Terrace Mountain. He spied Subhuti below.

"I can jump two miles in one leap," Monkey King shouted, waving his tail and puffing himself up.

"Please go ahead," the Master called to him.

Monkey put his feet together, drew a deep breath, made a mighty leap into the air, and landed about a mile away in a dark-leafed persimmon tree. He snatched a few persimmons and leaped back to where Subhuti was standing.

"Well, well, friend Monkey," Subhuti said. "I am afraid that you have much to learn."

Monkey looked surprised.

"A true space traveler crosses the four seas in one day. He crosses the Eastern Sea and the Southern Sea, and the Western Sea, and lands again in the Northern Sea."

Monkey's tail dropped.

"There's a great difference between jumping *willfully* the way you do and rising in the air through the power of the soul."

"Huh-uh?" Monkey said, lying down with his head between his paws.

"True Immortals sit with their legs crossed and rise straight to Heaven."

"Oh, but what must I do?" Monkey asked, sitting up again.

"Come down from your rock and listen closely. You shall learn the shooting star trick. Only remember, do not waste your powers on small matters."

Monkey King climbed down to listen.

"First make yourself absolutely still."

Monkey King couldn't stop wriggling.

"Pretend that you are a smooth lake without a ripple."

"I can't."

"Well then, find a comfortable position."

Monkey King stood on his head.

"Stay there," Subhuti commanded. "Don't come down."

"All right."

"Now whistle twice, click your tongue twice, and recite this spell." He leaned over and whispered a long saying into Monkey King's ear. "When you see the stars descending from the disk of the sun or the moon and you've recited my saying, you will rise without effort."

Monkey King concentrated hard on doing just what Subhuti had told him. He felt himself rising in the air. He turned a giant somersault and in one leap went zooming as far away as the Southern Sea. He streaked through the sky like a flaming meteor. He could have gone on forever if only he hadn't been so hungry. A gnawing in his stomach made him return to the Cave of the Crescent Moon and Three Stars.

Monkey King landed near the pine tree by the cave door just as Subhuti's pupils were bringing in batches of wild honey.

"How are you coming with all your lessons?" asked a friendly pupil.

"Oh fine. I practice all the time," Monkey King replied. "Could I just have some honey?"

"Of course."

Monkey King gobbled down a batch and tossed the empty honeycomb over his shoulder.

"Why don't you show us some of your latest magic?" the pupil asked.

Monkey King puffed himself up. "What shall I do for you?"

"Could you change into something for us?" asked another pupil.

"I know what I'll do," Monkey King said, closing his eyes. He recited the magic formula and changed into a pine tree exactly like the one in front of them. His form was tall and slim, and he had many waving green branches.

"Bravo!" they shouted, laughing and clapping their hands.

Monkey King changed back into his natural shape again, bowing and waving his tail. They roared with delight.

"I'll change into a speckled bustard if you like," Monkey King said, but out of the corner of his eye he saw Subhuti coming out of the cave, pounding his staff as he came.

"What is all this commotion?"

"Only a quiet game," Monkey King said,

stepping out from among the pupils. "Really nothing at all."

"Such screeching and carrying on. This is a holy place and a place for learning," Subhuti said solemnly.

"We beg your pardon, Reverend Master," a pupil said. "Monkey King was demonstrating his powers by becoming a pine tree. Perhaps we clapped too loudly."

Subhuti's face was full of anger. "Away all of you. I wish to speak to Monkey alone."

His pupils went inside the cave.

"Now Monkey, this cave is not a circus. You must leave the Cave of the Crescent Moon and Three Stars at once."

Monkey King gasped.

"Why did you use your powers so cheaply? What made you turn yourself into a pine tree?"

"I don't know," Monkey King said humbly.

"You used your magic to strut and show off. Great powers may only be used for great purposes."

"I am truly sorry," Monkey King said shaken. He swallowed hard.

"Being sorry is not enough. Don't you know

that all my pupils will try to force these secrets from you?"

Monkey King couldn't keep back his tears. "But what shall I do?" he asked sobbing.

"That's up to you," Subhuti replied. "Return to your home, I suppose."

"To the Cave of the Water Curtain?" Monkey King said slowly. He had lived there so long ago it was hard to remember. "But how can I ever thank you or repay you for all that you've done for me?" Monkey King's voice was weak.

"That is not necessary."

"But all you've taught me, like the secret of a long life, the shooting star trick, the way to change myself into—"

"All I ask is that you forget that I was the one who taught them to you. If you get into any more trouble, you are not to mention my name," Subhuti said firmly.

"Oh, don't worry," Monkey King said when he knew he had to leave. "I certainly won't."

"I taught you because of your unusual birth, and now all I can do is to mourn for your future, for you will surely get into trouble again."

Monkey King bowed low. "If anyone asks me about my new powers, I'll say that I learned them from a holy man. I won't tell anyone your name."

With this solemn pledge, Monkey King stood on his head, whistled twice, clicked his tongue twice, and recited the magic saying of Subhuti. He rose straight in the air, feet first. Turning a giant somersault, he soared through the sky toward the Eastern Sea.

4

The Dragon's Weapon

Down, down, Monkey King glided, now through clouds, now through misty vapors, looking for the Mountain of Flowers and Fruit. Cranes were crying to one another. Louder noises and wailing reached his ears. Was it the howling of jackals—in the daytime? The shrill screams of terrified monkeys brought Monkey King zooming to the ground. A blazing anger filled his chest, and he let out a savage cry. "Who is here by my cave?"

A green demon, monstrously ugly with nine heads, lunged toward him.

"I am," he roared, smoke pouring out of his nostrils.

"Whoah! Moldy demon, Knobby Knees. Do I hear your bones creaking with age?" Monkey King shouted, coming nearer.

"What a scabby-faced windbag!" Green Demon shouted back. "Mark well. I'll throw down my sword and kill you with my fists."

"Rejoice little monkeys, I have returned." Monkey King called, hurling himself like a rock at Green Demon's ribs and jumping away from his wild-swinging arms.

"Some puffball of a baboon!" roared Green Demon, striking Monkey King's shoulder a resounding blow. Monkey King reeled and fell back. In an instant he had curled himself into a ball and was rolling over and over on the ground. Then he leaped into the air and bit Green Demon's stomach. This made Green Demon so angry that he slashed at Monkey King's head. Monkey King ducked from the flashing sword point. The other monkeys screeched, but Monkey King darted out, plucking some hairs from his arm as he went.

"Transform," he shouted, and bit a few hairs

into small pieces. At once the hairs turned into hundreds of tiny monkeys. In a second they were swarming all over Green Demon—kicking him, biting his ears and toes, and pounding his many noses. The tumult of the tiny screaming monkeys so befuddled Green Demon's brain that he dropped his sword. White Monkey snatched it up. The tiny monkey army went on pulling Green Demon's hair and spitting in his eyes. Suddenly Green Demon fell down on his knees and his heads jerked back. Monkey King came in like a thunderbolt, cutting off those heads with his sword like a scythe cutting grass. Blood gushed forth and Green Demon sank to the ground.

Monkey King stood still for a moment. "Transform," he commanded. The army of tiny monkeys changed back into the hairs of his body. The Immortal Subhuti's multiplying trick had been well learned. Monkey King thought of his kindly teacher as he lay Green Demon's sword down on the ground.

His trusted ministers, Wise Monkey and Lazy Monkey, rushed to embrace him. Loud cries came from all the other monkeys as they poured out of the grotto with the blue-green walls.

"How long has this fellow been tormenting you?" Monkey King asked his ministers.

"Two years," Wise Monkey replied.

"What happened to our army?"

"We had bamboo spears and a few banners. We were like the praying mantis who lies in a rut and tries to stop the chariot by waving its forearms," Wise Monkey answered.

"Ah, my poor monkeys. To think that you suffered so. We must get strong weapons of iron and steel. But for now let us celebrate."

A banquet was quickly prepared on the stone tables in front of the grotto. The monkeys wined and dined and took turns doing homage to their king. Everyone wanted to know how Green Demon was slain and how it was that their great king had learned so much magic. Monkey King told them about his journey over two oceans and his years of instruction at the Cave of the Crescent Moon and Three Stars. The rejoicing lasted far into the night.

The next day Monkey King summoned Wise Monkey and Lazy Monkey to his council chamber. "You will start training our army," he told them. "That is first. But where can I find swords of steel, axes, and weapons of iron?" he demanded. Wise Monkey advised him that they could be found in the kingdom of Mo Yang.

Soon Monkey King was shown some weapons that had been made there, but they did not satisfy him. Once more he summoned Wise Monkey and Lazy Monkey to his council chamber.

"I am pleased with our army, and it is doing well," he said. "Never again will a hateful demon ravage our land."

The two trusted ministers nodded in agreement.

"But I am not content."

"You are often not content," Lazy Monkey remarked. "Why don't you relax, like me?"

"I can't find a weapon that is powerful enough," continued Monkey King.

"Great King," Wise Monkey said, "earthly arms will never suffice. If your magic still burns within you, perhaps you need a weapon with untold, hidden powers?"

Monkey King's tail twitched with curiosity.

"I am told that the water under the bridge

goes straight into the sea. It is rumored that the Dragon King of the Eastern Sea has—"

"You need say no more," Monkey King said, jumping up.

Monkey King bade his ministers farewell. He ran to the shining bridge. Reciting a formula to protect him from drowning, he waved his tail in the air and dove into the river. Down, down, down he swam into the blue-green depths. A garden of pink sea fans and waving green seaweed unfolded before his eyes. Three golden fish as large as porpoises swam over and under one another with a careless grace until they spied him.

"Stop," they cried, barring his way. "Announce yourself, for you are approaching the territory of the Dragon King of the Eastern Sea."

"I am Monkey King from the Mountain of Flowers and Fruit and a neighbor of yours. Show me to your king."

The huge golden fish beckoned with their fins for Monkey King to follow and led him to a crystal palace and through a dozen chambers to the throne room. Dragon King, splendid in his scales of shimmering green and gold, greeted

him pompously and suggested that they have tea together in the coral garden.

As they drank, Dragon King looked down his long nose at Monkey King. "What is your mission?" he asked in a throaty voice. Monkey King explained how the Green Demon had attacked his kingdom and asked Dragon King for a weapon with hidden powers. He guzzled his tea and put his cup over his nose to drain it. "I am sure you must have something," he concluded.

"Possibly." Dragon King commanded a perch captain to bring a nine-pronged fork, which Monkey King turned down as being too feeble. Then he offered a battle-ax weighing seven thousand pounds.

"Too light for me," Monkey King said, thrusting it into the air and throwing it over his shoulder.

Dragon King turned pale green. "More tea?"

"Certainly," Monkey King said, handing him his cup.

"I'm afraid that is the heaviest weapon we have."

Monkey King drained his cup in one huge gulp. "Better look once more."

Dragon King turned aside to consult with the Keeper of the Sea Treasury. Then he turned back to Monkey King. "There is one other possibility. In our treasury is a strange, long object which has been glowing with a weird light these past few weeks. It is much too heavy to move. Perhaps you would like to see it. Keeper of the Treasury, guide our neighbor there."

In a few minutes Monkey King returned, prancing about, slicing the air with his new weapon, and scaring all the dragon princes and turtle messengers. Dragon King clutched his chair. His voice shook. "One of my ancestors used it to see how deep the oceans were. He hoped its great weight would calm the seas. I thought it weighed over thirteen thousand pounds."

"It does," Monkey King said, flourishing it in the air. It glowed as he did so, making an arc of fire in front of them. "It was twenty feet long and a bit clumsy, so I had to make it shorter." Monkey King said smiling. "Much obliged. I'll take it."

"It was really nothing," Dragon King said nervously.

"Oh yes, one more thing. Do you have a fine coat of mail to go with the magic weapon? I feel almost naked without something to match it."

At first Dragon King said he had nothing, but Monkey King threatened him with his new weapon.

"Easy. Ah. Don't be in such a h-hurry. I'll just call my dragon brothers," Dragon King said hastily.

The alarm was sounded. In a trice, three dragons arrived at the palace. Dragon King left Monkey King to greet them and quickly explained that a monkey with magic powers was threatening his life for a coat of mail.

"Oh, I can give him a coat of mail," the Dragon King of the Western Sea said. "From what you say, it may be wise to weight him down with gifts."

"Nonsense, he should be punished, the Jade Emperor ought to know about this." said the Dragon of the Eastern Sea.

The dragon brothers were brought to see Monkey King. The Dragon of the Northern Sea offered him a pair of cloud-walking shoes, and the other dragons presented Monkey King with a purple and gold cap of phoenix feathers and a golden coat of mail. Monkey King put them on and was just feeling his toes in the cloud-walking shoes when the dragons stretched out their long necks and pressed their faces to his. "Aren't you going to thank us?" they said, hissing like tea kettles.

That was too much for Monkey King. "Thank you, thank you, thank you," he said, swiping their ears and their scaly tails with his fiery weapon.

They drew back in terror. "Don't think that you can get away with it. You'll see. We'll report you to the Jade Emperor, the Supreme Ruler of Heaven."

"What a bunch of tattletails," Monkey King said to the dragons. "I was just playing."

"Ssss. You played with the wrong dragons, little ape," they said, hissing again. "Remember, the Jade Emperor is the Supreme Ruler of the Earth, the Sea, and all thirty- three Heavens."

"Can't you take a joke?" Monkey King asked. He made a face and strode out. "Oh, oh, I had better hurry home," he said to himself.

Monkey King swam back to the bridge. His golden suit of mail shone in the sun as he climbed out of the river. His suit and plumed cap were dry. Wise Monkey and Lazy Monkey bowed. Monkey King began to feel better. He gripped his powerful weapon and commanded them to follow him to his council chamber.

"Look at my new weapon," Monkey King said, setting it down so the golden band at the tip touched the floor.

"Oh, let us try it, please," Lazy Monkey said.

The two monkeys tried to lift the weapon. Amazement spread over their faces when it wouldn't budge. They sucked in their breath and bit their tails.

"Ah, but it is no ordinary weapon. The Dragon of the Eastern Sea told me that it had once been used to measure the ocean. It was too long when I first saw it, so I made it smaller," Monkey King said, picking it up and waving it in the air.

"Smaller, smaller," he commanded. Presto! It was so little that Monkey King popped it behind his ear like a pencil. The monkeys hooted and jumped up and down.

"More tricks," they cried, clapping their hands.

Monkey took his pencil and placed it upright in his hand. "Larger, larger," he ordered, and the weapon grew tall like a spear. Monkey got up and ran with it to the bridge. "Taller, taller, taller," he cried until it swelled to the size of a giant tree. Monkey grew with it. "Taller, taller," he roared, and the weapon shot up into the clouds. Monkey King grew so tall that his head looked down on Tai Mountain and his shoulders were in the clouds, too.

From this height he looked up to a golden cloud slowly descending from the Southern Gate of Heaven. "Oh, Oh! Have I gone too far? There cannot be two suns in the sky," he said to himself, using the ancient proverb. He had a sinking feeling in his vitals. Maybe the dragon kings had told on him after all.

"Smaller, smaller, smaller, smaller— and hurry," he cried until his weapon shrank to the size of a mountain, the size of a tree, the size of a spear, and finally the size of a pencil. Quickly he put it behind his ear and ran back to the council chamber. He was still dizzy when a messenger announced that a strange ambassador had just arrived.

"What's his name? What does he look like?"

Monkey King asked sharply.

"He calls himself the Great White Star. His face has so many wrinkles you can't see his eyes. He has long white hair and—"

"Where's he from?" Monkey queried.

"He says he's from Heaven."

"Oh, oh," Monkey King said, scratching his head. "I can see trouble coming."

5

The Great Sage

Monkey King was lucky that it was the Great White Star who was assigned to be his guardian and to take him to Heaven. White Star was wrinkled enough to be old, old enough to be wise, and wise enough to be full of humor. In short, he was a fine mixture of bubble and sagacity.

On their way to the Jade Emperor, Great White Star tried to prepare Monkey King for his audience.

Did Monkey King know that he must bow twenty times before the Jade Emperor?

Did Monkey know that he must fix his gaze no higher than the Jade Emperor's knee?

Did Monkey know that he must never speak before being spoken to?

No. Monkey King knew none of these things, and he wasn't paying attention to Great White Star. He was busy cleaning his silvery fur coat.

"Monkey, are you listening? It is all very well to cut capers on earth, but you are going to see the Jade Emperor, the Supreme Ruler of Heaven."

Monkey King parted the hair on his stomach with his fingers and peered at the pink skin underneath.

"He is second only to the Lord Buddha. Monkey, the Lord Buddha is the Supreme Ruler of the entire Universe."

Monkey King gazed off into the distance.

"This is no time for cloud gazing. We are almost at the Heavenly Gates."

Monkey King's eyes grew larger and larger as they passed through the Heavenly Gates and past the pool of green jade with all its fountains to the palace where the famous Lao Tzu lived. His guardian told Monkey King all about Lao Tzu's Golden Elixir of Long Life and pointed out his laboratory. They went past the treasury hall and dozens of other buildings with names like the Palace of Surpassing Brightness, the Pavilion of Favorable Winds, and the Hall of Magic Mists. Monkey King couldn't possibly keep them all straight.

When the time came for Monkey King's audience with the Jade Emperor, Monkey King forgot all the things he was supposed to do. The first minister asked who had offended the Dragon Kings of the Four Seas and taken their most precious weapon.

Monkey King bowed and said, "It's me."

The court was horrified. However, the Jade Emperor was kind to Monkey King, saying that he would learn the ways of Heaven in time.

There was more urgent business at hand. No one quite knew what to do with Monkey King, and the only job available was in the royal stables. It wasn't what Monkey King had expected at all.

He hadn't been there very long before he discovered that he had been given a lowly assignment with no salary and that he simply didn't count for much in Heaven. What did this punishment mean?

The more Monkey King thought about it, the more furious he became. At last he couldn't stand it any longer. He rushed off to the Southern Gate of Heaven, thumbing his nose at the guards as he went through.

"What an insult!" he shouted as he prepared for his flight back to earth. He rose straight in the air, feet first, turned a giant somersault, and went streaking off through the sky.

After a while, Monkey King neared his beloved mountain. At the very top, he could see swarms of monkeys putting the finishing touches on a red pagoda. He lowered himself slowly into their midst. Loud cries of joy surrounded him. "Great King, we welcome you."

"What grand surprise is this?" Monkey King asked looking at his new garden house.

"We just finished this red pagoda." Wise Monkey answered. "We didn't know when you'd be back this time. Look! We've even dedicated it to you. Lazy Monkey made it up. See? 'To the Great Sage.' That is because you have learned so much from the holy man."

Monkey King read the entire inscription

aloud. "To the Great Sage, Equal of Heaven."
He shrugged his shoulders.

"Well, you *were* up in Heaven for a long time," Wise Monkey said, "so we figured you were equal to them."

"But I was only there for two weeks," Monkey King insisted.

"Ah, but time must be different up there. A day in Heaven must be a year on earth," Wise Monkey replied.

"You do look older, Wise Monkey. But come, let us celebrate our new pagoda and my return. Have you changed, too, Lazy Monkey?"

Lazy Monkey wanted to tell him that he didn't eat so much anymore, but he didn't have a chance. Monkey King was full of tales about Heaven. They drank rice wine and coconut wine and made merry under the eaves of the red pagoda. Lazy Monkey made up a ditty—

> Through the lips and around the gums
> Look out stomach, here it comes.

—but he was careful not to drink as much as he used to.

Monkey King was inspecting his kingdom

the next day, and everywhere he went he saw red and yellow banners emblazoned with the words "The Great Sage, Equal of Heaven." The more he thought about it, the more he liked it. In fact, it rather made up for that lowly job he had been given at the royal stables. Monkey King had almost completed his tour when a messenger accosted him.

"Well?" he asked.

The messenger explained that he had just come down from Heaven.

"And?"

"Prince Natha is on his way to arrest you for deserting your post in Heaven."

"Who does he think he is?" Monkey King demanded. "Bring me my armor," he said to Lazy Monkey, who brought it at once.

Hurriedly Monkey King put on his new gold and purple cap, his golden suit of mail, and his cloud-walking shoes. "Show me to him," he shouted, grabbing his fiery weapon.

The time for battle came all too quickly. Monkey King went forth to meet the handsome Prince Natha who had arrived at the walls of the kingdom.

"Who are you to crash my gate?" Monkey

King said, fuming. He turned a blazing eye on the prince. "What shabby deity is it now? Oh, so it is little Prince Natha. I'll spare your life on one condition. Do you see my new title on the red and yellow banners above your head?"

Prince Natha looked up.

"If the Jade Emperor agrees to my new title, all will be well. But tell your emperor that if he refuses, my monkeys and I will batter down his palace."

"Silly ape," responded the handsome prince, laughing. "What arrogance! One blow of my sword and you will be dead," and he swung at Monkey King's head.

"Is this all you can do, little prince?" Monkey King met his blow with the dragon's weapon.

They stormed over the mountainside, hurling insults and exchanging sharp blows. The prince's magic was very strong. When it looked as if Monkey King might have the edge, Prince Natha changed into a three-headed god with six arms and a different weapon in each arm. He brought all six weapons down on Monkey King at once. Monkey King dodged out from under, took a turn with his own magic and

became a three-headed, six-armed monkey with six weapons. They fought halfway up and halfway down the sky, but neither was able to catch the other unaware.

Both of them grew tired of so many arms, legs, and weapons. Monkey King changed back into his monkey body again. With a flick-of-a-flash, Monkey King lifted his fiery weapon and brought it crashing down onto the prince's shoulders. Natha was so busy thinking up new magic that he didn't have time to escape the blow. Monkey King's stroke sent the prince reeling, and Natha sank to the ground.

"That trip to the sea dragon was worth it," Monkey King said to himself. "They'll never get me now."

Monkey returned to his ministers in his cave. He ordered the guard of monkeys protecting his kingdom to be doubled.

"This may well be a beginning," he said, taking off his armor. "I need a rest. Bring me some peaches by the bridge."

Monkey King flopped down in a stone chair with the blue-green grotto at his back. He ate twenty-five peaches. Then he became drowsy and slept until the next morning. He was scarcely awake when Great White Star appeared at the gates of his kingdom.

"Well, well," Monkey King said, yawning, when Wise Monkey announced his coming. "He's probably going to offer me something better this time. Bring him around with a proper escort."

In a few minutes Great White Star arrived. Monkey King jumped up when he saw him. "Greetings, Old Star. Forgive me for not coming out to meet you. Do sit down."

"Thank you," Great White Star replied, joining him on a stone chair. "The Jade Emperor asked me to come. He was informed that you were unhappy with your appointment in Heaven. At first the Jade Emperor just couldn't understand your complaint. After all, as the Jade Emperor often says, "All officials proceed from lesser to more important appointments.""

Monkey King made a wry face.

"The Jade Emperor sent Prince Natha to subdue you, and when he failed to do so, it was proposed to send a whole army."

Monkey King nodded. "I thought that might happen."

"I was against this. War is never a solution to difficult problems," Great White Star said gravely. "I put in a good word for you."

"Ha ha, thank you, Old Star," Monkey said, swinging his tail back and forth.

"The Jade Emperor has agreed to accept your new title. Of course, it doesn't fit any of our catagories."

"To tell you the truth, one of my monkeys made it up. I suppose there really isn't such a thing."

New lines appeared on Great White Star's face as he gazed from among his many wrinkles at Monkey King. "The Jade Emperor has also decided to give you a new job," he said solemnly.

"Oh, what is it?"

"You are to look after the peach orchards. It's an important post."

"Ah!" Monkey King smiled, rubbing his stomach. "I love peaches."

"But these are not ordinary peaches, Monkey. They are the most precious peaches of immortality."

"All the better," said Monkey King.

6

The Havoc of Monkey

"Where is Monkey King?" asked one of the
fairy maidens who arrived at the peach orchard
to fill her baskets for the annual peach banquet.

"Where is Monkey King?" asked a second
maiden.

"You might try looking in the orchard,
where the peaches of immortality grow, not
telling her that Monkey's clothes lay on the
ground under the greatest treasure of them
all—a tree whose fruit ripens once in nine
thousand years."

"Monkey! Monkey King!" they called as
they came to the mellow quiet of the peach

trees. The fair maidens ran back and forth under the trees of immortality, bending the lowest boughs and filling their baskets. Except for the droning of the bees, the whole world seemed to be asleep. Then one of the maidens noticed some plump peaches with unusual purple markings in the back row of trees. She spied Monkey's robe underneath one of them. As luck would have it, she pulled on the very limb where Monkey King had made himself into a two-inch monkey and fallen asleep. The sudden jerk woke him up in a hurry. He changed back to his usual size and dropped down to the ground crying out, "What are you doing here? What an intrusion! Who are you, anyway?"

"Great Sage, Equal of Heaven," the young maiden said, kneeling at his feet, "we are here to gather peaches for the annual peach banquet."

"I see," Monkey King said, curling his tail.

"The annual banquet is tomorrow at the treasury tower. We talked to that old guard at your gates. He said to look for you in the orchard and—"

"Hmmm," Monkey King began to think. There was a sudden gleam in his eye. A sort of I-would-like-to-go-too gleam.

"Oh that is perfectly all right. Whatever can I do to help?" Monkey King paused. "This peach banquet. Tell me, is everyone invited?" Monkey King asked, licking his lips.

"It is the biggest social event in Heaven," she replied. "The Buddha of the Western Heaven and Kuan Yin, Goddess of Mercy, and I don't know who else. They are the most important ones, but let us go back to my friend. She'll know all about it."

When they rejoined the other maiden, Monkey King asked again about invitations for the annual peach banquet.

"All the Immortals of the Ten Continents come," said the second maiden. "And the Princes of the Five Planets and the Dragon Kings of the Four Seas and the Nine Guardians of the Heavenly Gates," she continued.

"That is funny. My invitation has not come yet," Monkey King said. "There's probably been some slip-up somewhere."

"We haven't heard of any. Of course, there

are time-honored rules." she paused. "We know last year's guest list, but we don't know if there have been any changes."

"Of course not. Perhaps you can help me then. If you will just stay here a few moments, I will inquire and see where my invitation is," Monkey King said quietly.

Before the maidens knew what was happening, Monkey King recited a special formula which was a four-hour fixing spell.

"Stay, stay, stay wherever you are," he cried.

The maidens stood fixed like statues, unable even to move their eyes. Monkey King kicked up his heels and was off. Everything was going well for Monkey King and he sang as he trotted along, feeling himself very clever indeed.

Preparations for the banquet were well under way when he arrived at the treasury tower. He looked inside to see many bustling servants filling goblets with jade- and ruby-colored wine and putting them on the long, shining tables of the golden banquet hall. Such a delicious wine aroma filled his nostrils! Monkey King made little hiccuping sighs of delight as another prank formed in his fertile brain.

He sat down on a bench in the banquet hall and took a fistful of the finest white fur from his stomach. Putting it in his mouth, he said a magic-changing spell which made all the hundreds of hairs turn into hundreds of gray moths. Almost immediately the gray moths of sleep settled on the eyelids of the servants, causing them to sink to the floor. Heads resting on their chests, they fell into a deep sleep.

When Monkey King was sure that his sleeping magic had taken effect, he drank from one of the jugs. "Tastes like lovely firewater," he sang. He tilted another wine jug and drank deeply. Several jars later, he spied a long empty table whose surface shone like glass. He jumped up on it and slid on his back, pumping with his legs the length of the table. Then with broad swimming movements, he crawled all the way to the other end on his stomach.

Monkey was gloriously drunk.

He hopped down off the table, uncorked some more wine jugs, threw the corks in the air, and began sampling some of the good things to eat. "Excellent bean cakes," he remarked. "Oh, and here are some fine wine jugs for Wise Monkey and Lazy Monkey. I'll just tuck them under my arms. La, dee, dah, I am beginning to feel such shivers of happiness I am," and he ran out to the fountains of the jade green pool. In and out of the splashing water he danced with a song on his lips. "What was Lazy Monkey's ditty? Oh yes."

Through the lips and around the gums
Look out stomach, here it comes.

Whether it was the shock of the icy water or not, Monkey King suddenly began to feel ill. Truly wretched. Not a bit like his usual self. Poor Monkey King staggered along with his head spinning. He lost his way. One shining hall of light looked just like another shining hall of light. The names were so much fluff in his head.

After a while, he came to and realized that the marble building ahead of him was the palace where the famous Lao Tzu lived and had his laboratory. Subhuti had once talked to him. "Wasn't it Lao Tzu's sacred formula of long life that Subhuti gave me?" Monkey King said to himself. Great White Star said that he had a new Golden Elixir that made you live forever.

Monkey King wandered around until he

found Lao Tzu's laboratory. No one was there. He set down his wine jugs in the doorway and wrinkled up his small nose. What sharp, bewitching smells!

"How splendid!" Monkey King said to himself, glancing at the mysterious chemicals bubbling away on little stoves.

"A chance in a million," he whispered.

"Two million," he muttered half-aloud.

"Somewhere," Monkey King sputtered, "is the highest treasure of the Immortals. Just look at all the pans of burning elixirs. I was going to make some magic stuff like that myself once, but I never did."

Monkey King jumped on one foot and then the other, shouting "hoo, hooo, heee" as he danced around the laboratory.

"What is this shining silver stuff?" Monkey King said aloud. "It looks so good. I'll just try some and see what it tastes like." He picked up a wide-mouthed jar, threw back his head, and swallowed. The elixir slid down his throat and landed like a hard ball in his stomach. He made an odd bleating sound. His stomach felt heavy, very heavy. "That couldn't be Lao Tzu's Golden Elixir. No sir," he said to himself. "Better try something else." Oh, but his stomach felt like a ton of lead.

What was that against the wall by the window? Jars of blue and green vitriol sparkled from the shelves. Pans of saltpeter, charcoal, red cinnebar, and lead were nearby on a low table. He stood in front of them trying desperately to think. Where, oh where was the Golden Elixir?

A fine gray substance beckoned from a gleaming round tray. He took a taste, but it was so hideous that he threw it in a brazier full of a bubbling gray-black mass. Wham! Bang! Boom! An explosion sent him flying to the other end of the laboratory.

Monkey King picked himself up slowly. "Bad, bad," he said to himself. "I am at the bottom. I have known great heights. Once I even solved all the secrets of alchemy. Ah me, the Golden Elixir. I've got to find it before someone comes."

He heard a noise outside the laboratory.

"Quick. Here is some golden powder in a gourd. It has a nice smell." He sniffed again and wrinkled up his nose. Then he tilted the gourd back and swallowed everything as if it was nothing but roasted beans. He downed five other gourds just like it. Hmm. Delicious. He felt fine until a burning sensation, not just here and there, flowed through his whole body. His head felt like the inside of a clanging bell. His shoulders began to swell. A strange power ran through him, bringing a surge of high spirits and towering energy. "It must have been the Golden Elixir! If the Jade Emperor finds out, I am lost. Run, run, run. I'll just hurry down to my nice world below."

Monkey King skipped out the door, banging and almost tipping over one of the wine jugs he was planning to take to his monkeys. He scooped up both jugs and bolted out of Lao Tzu's laboratory. This time he couldn't afford to meet anyone, so he made himself invisible. Monkey King whisked by the Western Gate of Heaven and prepared for his flight back to earth. He rose straight in the air, feet first, turned a giant somersault, and streaked away through the sky. Soaring, soaring, soaring, he began to feel like a mighty rocket, ready to shower the heavens with glorious red and green stars! Such power and glory! He thought of Subhuti. What would his master think of

him now? He soared past the bright stars, the cloudy meteors, the moon itself. Lovely moon. Did she have a rabbit inside her? Was she a lady? Some time he would go and see for himself. Down, down, down, down he went.

When he arrived at his beloved mountain, it was dusk. The first person he met was Lazy Monkey. Monkey King greeted him warmly, handing him the precious wine jugs. "I have something for you. Take them to the peach courtyard where nothing will happen to them. I will meet you there."

Lazy Monkey disappeared amidst the loud hurrahs of all the happy monkeys. "Our King, our King is back! Hooray! Hooray!" The little monkeys jumped in the trees and perched on the branches to get a better view.

"Monkeys, dear monkeys, how glad I am to see you," Monkey King exclaimed, going about among them. "Go on with your fun and games," he said finally "and I will join you shortly for a feast."

On the way to the peach courtyard, he met Wise Monkey, who embraced him with tears in his eyes. "I didn't think you would come back this time," he sighed.

Lazy Monkey was smelling the jug of red wine as they entered. Monkey explained that it was more precious than rubies. "It is for you, Lazy Monkey. Half a cupful and you'll live a hundred years."

"A hundred years?" echoed Lazy Monkey, hopping up and down.

Monkey King picked up the other jug. "This is even more precious than jade, Wise Monkey. It is the most valuable wine of all. May you live for five hundred years!"

"Wine from Heaven? I don't deserve it. How we have missed you," Wise Monkey babbled. "I can't believe it." He didn't say everything at once but with much sighing and weeping.

"Come, come," Monkey King said. "Drink it quickly. We must join the others."

Raising their jugs, his trusted ministers drank long and smacked their lips. Monkey King left them as they were rubbing their stomachs around and around with dazed looks on their faces. He went to his usual place at the end of the long stone table. Everyone crowded around. Monkey King asked his generals how the army was getting on, but he didn't give them time to reply.

"We may have a little trouble later, but let's enjoy one another now," he said, raising his stone cup. "Our glory can wait. And now three cheers for Wise Monkey, friend and ruler, who has managed so well while I have been gone."

Loud cries went up from the throng. Cups and plates flew in the air. Monkey King forgot all about his foolish misdeeds in Heaven, and he was glad to be home again—home by the river, home by the hump-backed bridge and their grotto with blue-green walls, and best of all, home with his own kind. What greater joy could there be than feasting with his own dear monkeys?

7

The Forces of Heaven

The trail of Monkey King's havoc, the full flowering of his mischief, became known in Heaven. The fairy maidens from the peach orchard, the winemakers, the breathless officials, complained to the Jade Emperor. And when the emperor himself went out to greet the illustrious Lao Tzu and heard that Monkey King had stolen the elixer of life he had worked on for so many years, he was very grave indeed. To make matters worse, hardly had the emperor returned to his throne than Great White Star arrived and asked to be relieved of his post.

"This has gone too far," the emperor said. "Summon a council of war. Call my generals, Prince Natha, General Ravan, the Kings of the Four Quarters," he commanded.

The emperor's ministers arrived promptly in the council room. Justice would be done at last. The head-nodding of his ministers and the firm lines around their mouths said so. Everyone had had quite enough. Monkey King was due for his comeuppance.

The first minister looked down his nose. "Monkey has broken the law."

"Hear, hear," they all said, pounding the table. "We are agreed."

"Now you must discuss strategy," said the Jade Emperor.

"I will marshall the twenty-eight Constellations, the nine Heavenly Fires, the twelve Hours, and all the Stars along with the one hundred thousand Heavenly Forces," General Ravan began. "First we will surround the Mountain of Flowers and Fruit."

"And stamp on his mountain until it is flat," shouted Prince Natha, who was eager to get even with Monkey King. "And I will smash his cave to bits and kill all his subjects."

"You two sort this out between you. But remember, you must capture this fighting monkey alive."

For all his brave talk, Prince Natha returned two days later to report to the emperor that one hundred thousand Heavenly Forces could not capture him. His monkey army fought bravely, and thousands were killed. Monkey King himself was here, there, and everywhere. The Heavenly Forces had struck, but just when they thought they had him, he was nowhere to be seen.

The emperor was stunned, but he recovered quickly. "Then I will talk with the compassionate Kuan Yin, whom I have just appointed as Monkey's new guardian. Where your forces have failed, the power of her wisdom may prevail."

Accordingly, Kuan Yin was summoned to the throne. The emperor had forgotten how beautiful she was—tall and willowy, with black hair, almond eyes, and a face as pale as the whitest jade.

Kuan Yin bowed, pressing the palms of her hands together. The Jade Emperor explained his plight. She listened quietly.

"Your majesty need not be troubled, for I know of someone who can catch your monkey."

"Someone in Heaven?"

"No, the illustrious Ehr-lang, your nephew, the magician who lives with his brothers at Kuan River."

"Send for him at once," the emperor said, waving his jade fan. "Is he the one who is always storming about with his giant pitchforks?"

"Yes, but he is proud. If you order him to come, he will refuse," Kuan Yin said softly. "Therefore, you must humble yourself and ask him to help you."

Immediately a messenger was dispatched with an appeal. He returned late in the day saying that Ehr-lang would arrive the next day and that he could hardly wait to capture Monkey King. As swift as a dream, Ehr-lang and his brothers flew to General Ravan's camp. Although Ehr-lang was very handsome, he had disguised himself to look like a devil, with streaming red hair, drooping fangs, and lidless eyes that glowed like hot coals. The general showed Ehr-lang and his ugly brothers where his troops were stationed outside Monkey King's gates. After he explained his strategy, he reported that Monkey King was probably inside his cave resting from their last battle.

In turn, Ehr-lang gave last-minute instructions to the general. "Don't worry about what goes on in the heavens, but there's one thing you must do without fail. Here is a Mirror of Truth. Stand with it halfway up the sky. If Monkey tries to hide, watch his reflection in this magic mirror. Whatever you do, don't lose sight of him."

"Anything else?" asked General Ravan.

"No."

As Ehr-lang approached the gates of Monkey King's kingdom, he noticed the red and yellow banners with Monkey's title—Great Sage, Equal of Heaven. "What nerve!" he snarled when he saw their inscription. "Hah! What does that baboon think he is doing? Tickling the tiger's nose with a straw?"

Monkey King ran out of his cave to meet Ehr-lang. He swung his fiery weapon in the air shouting "What bald-headed donkey, what slobberer of salvation is it this time?"

"Don't you have eyes in your silly head? Do

you fail to recognize me, the Jade Emperor's nephew? I've come to skin you alive, you nauseating ape."

"Oh, Ehr-lang, somehow your face didn't stick in my mind. I remember now, you used to have *one* stomach and just one chin," Monkey said chuckling.

"Son of a turtle, I'll bury my white blade in you and bring out a red one." Ehr-lang lunged.

Monkey King ducked. "You snaggle-toothed booby," he yelled.

They circled around one another.

"Your tongue is sharp, but not half as sharp as my pitchfork," Ehr-lang roared as he hurled it at Monkey King's chest. Monkey King's fiery weapon barred the way. The fighting grew fiercer.

Suddenly Ehr-lang rose up like a black cloud in the sky and, using his magic, turned into a monster one hundred thousand feet high. His two arms, each holding a giant pitchfork, were like thunderbolts. His flaming red hair swept the sky, his face turned blue, his lidless eyes smouldered, and his mouth foamed. So monstrous was Ehr-lang, that Monkey King's generals trembled. His officers threw down their

arms and his army fled as chickens scatter when a fox raids their coop in the night.

Monkey King changed into an enormous monkey as tall as Ehr-lang. The monster aimed a terrible blow at Monkey King's head. Monkey King dodged. Ehr-lang charged. Showers of sparks filled the sky. Over three hundred times they clashed. At last Ehr-lang changed back to his normal size. Monkey followed suit. And then he quailed. He saw that his army had left him. Monkey King had to do something quickly.

Down to the river slipped Monkey King and changed into a fish in the water. Down to the riverbank rushed Ehr-lang's brothers. Ehr-lang hurried to the bridge. "What's he done now? He's probably a fish or a shellfish," he said, looking down into the swirling waters. "I'll fool him."

Ehr-Lang transformed himself into a blue cormorant and skimmed over the surface of the river.

Monkey-now-Fish swam under a rock ledge. He gave his tail a swish as he looked up toward the sky. A bird was hovering over him. "It has the blue of a fish hawk," Monkey said to himself, diving down deeper, "but its plumage is not dark enough."

Monkey-now-Fish swam up to have another look. "It's just like a heron, but it has no crest on its head." He gave a cunning flip of his tail.

"It could be a stork," Monkey said, "but its feet and legs aren't red. Oh no! It's Ehr-lang." Monkey darted away, letting out a few bubbles as he went.

"Hmmm. That fish releasing bubbles," Ehr-lang said to himself, "could be a goldfish, but its tail isn't red. Or, it might be a trout, but I don't see any spots on its scales. Is it a perch? No, there aren't any spines on its head. Maybe it's a bass. Wait a minute. Why did it go darting away like that? Oh, nooo!" he groaned. "That was Monkey!"

In a twinkling, Monkey King had whisked himself out of the river and changed into a large speckled bustard. He flew up in the air, soaring over the hillside over the Cave of the Water Curtain. Ehr-lang changed into his old self again and shot at the bustard with his bow and arrow. He hit its tail, sending Monkey King falling to earth. Monkey King rolled and rolled and rolled down the hillside until he

landed halfway down in a scrubby bush. Ehr-lang started up the mountain to fetch his prey.

Monkey King had a second to change into something else. This time he became a wayside temple.

The round door to the temple was his grinning mouth.

The hinged doors were his teeth.

The guardian of the temple was his tongue.

The two little windows in the door were his eyes.

But what to do with his tail? Ehr-lang was almost upon him, so Monkey King stuck his tail up the back of the temple as a flagpole.

Ehr-Lang stopped at the small temple. He looked at the little door opening, at the hinged doors, and at the guardian of the temple. Then he laughed.

"I've seen a good many temples but never one with a flagpole." he said, laughing again. "I can't decide whether to poke out his eyes by smashing the windows, yank the whole thing out of the ground, or break his teeth by kicking in the doors!"

Monkey King trembled inside.

"Maybe I'll just give that pole-tail a good hard pull."

This was too much for Monkey King. He quickly took a giant leap into the air and disappeared from sight.

Just then two of Ehr-lang's brothers came to the scrubby bush asking where Monkey was.

"He was here a minute ago," Ehr-lang said, "pretending he was some sort of a wayside temple. You stay here on the hillside while I go up in the sky and look for him. I've had enough of this nonsense."

Ehr-lang mounted the cloud bank. Halfway up the sky he ran into General Ravan and his handsome son, Prince Natha.

"Have you seen that wicked ape anywhere?" he asked.

"No. My son Natha has been holding the Mirror of Truth, and I've been keeping watch," General Ravan replied.

"I don't envy you one bit," Prince Natha remarked. "I fought that stupid monkey up and down the sky myself." He glanced back at the mirror again. "Hold everything," Prince Natha said excitedly.

"Let me see," General Ravan shouted, coming to the prince's side. "Hurry up, Ehr-lang. That monkey has become invisible and is going as fast as he can to your river!"

It was true. Monkey King was flying straight toward Ehr-lang's temple at Kuan River. On the way, he made his face a bright blue, his hair and body red, his teeth pointed, and took the lids off his eyes. Monkey King now looked so much like Ehr-lang that Ehr-lang's guardian demons bowed low and let him enter their master's temple.

Monkey King sniffed the incense that filled the temple. He drew in his nostrils and inhaled deeply. What was it? He sniffed again. The smell of sandalwood, a spicy smell that took him back to the Cave of the Crescent Moon and Three Stars. He closed his eyes and thought of Subhuti. He opened them again when a messenger announced that another Ehr-lang had arrived.

Before Monkey King could escape, the real Ehr-lang stepped inside the main hall. "How dare that nauseating ape come here?" he shouted as he stormed about looking for Monkey King.

Monkey King hid behind a pillar and edged

his way toward the door changing back into his true form as he went. Then he scooted out of the cave, dodging Ehr-lang's blows.

Ehr-lang was furious. Fouling the air with his curses, he chased after Monkey King, speeding with the wind until he caught up with him at the Mountain of Flowers and Fruit. His brothers had almost cornered Monkey King with their dogs by the time he arrived.

It was true that Ehr-lang and his ugly brothers might have captured Monkey King this time anyway, but they had unexpected help. Up in the sky the dignitaries of Heaven were watching their battle from the Southern Gate. Lao Tzu remembered the time Monkey King wrecked his laboratory and ate his precious elixer. He cast a noose of molten steel in Monkey King's direction. Down, down, down it sailed, straight onto Monkey King's head. Alas, Monkey King was so busy with Ehr-lang, his brothers, and their dogs that he didn't see anything coming.

The metal noose slipped over him, and Ehr-lang's dogs rushed in. The biggest hound threw himself on top of Monkey King while the smaller ones nipped at his tail, his ears, his feet, wherever they could take hold. This was the end of the fight. Ehr-lang called off his dog pack, tied up Monkey King and stuck a blade in his lute bone so that he could no longer transform himself.

Monkey King's bag of tricks was empty.

"You're in for your punishment now, little monkey, swaggering bully," Ehr-lang said, taking the prisoner under his arm.

"Let me bid farewell to my monkeys," pleaded Monkey King.

"Some other time. We're off to Heaven, you and I. We've had more than enough of your insolence."

"Goodbye. Goodbye Lazy Monkey and Wise Monkey. Goodbye everyone," Monkey King called as they rose in the sky.

8

The Wager

The prisoner grunted in the small dark place. "What are you going to do with me?" he called from inside Lao Tzu's crucible of iron.

"I think I will cook you a little," replied Lao Tzu who had a head like an owl with the same blinking eyes. He wore a blue robe with zodiac signs on his wide sleeves. His quiet ways gave no hint of his famous reputation.

"You don't expect to get rid of me that way. A long time ago a holy man told me your sacred formula for long life," Monkey King called out from underneath the heavy iron lid.

"That was nice of him," Lao Tzu said, looking at his charge with a kindly air and blinking. "I think I can recover my elixir of immortality from you all right. After that it is up to the Jade Emperor."

Monkey called out again. "But you can't destroy me, I have double immortality. I ate half the peaches that make one live forever. I'll outlast all of you, you'll see."

"Not likely," Lao Tzu replied, but his mild voice was friendly. In fact, Monkey King couldn't help but like him.

Lao Tzu tapped the side of the crucible with his rod. His servant pumped the bellows until the coals glowed a fiery red. "Such a devil that monkey is," Lao Tzu said to himself. "Though I rather admire his courage."

Monkey King called again from inside the crucible. "Where's my guardian, Great White Star? I haven't seen him lately."

"He has another assignment. Kuan Yin has taken his place."

"Who's she?"

"She's the Goddess of Mercy," replied Lao Tzu.

"Oh yes, I remember now. I'd like to meet her."

"She's conferring with the Lord Buddha, Supreme Ruler of the Universe. Now that's enough little monkey. You must be warming up by now. It's time to see if the experiment works. Forty-nine days of cooking to get the elixir out of you," Lao Tzu mumbled. And he left Monkey King to roast.

"Forty-nine days of quiet in Heaven. Everyone was glad to enjoy a time of peace once more. The Jade Emperor made his customary rounds in his jewel-studded chariot. It was hard to remember the ill-fated peach festival and all the trouble Monkey King had caused. But, of course, the forty-ninth day arrived. Lao Tzu made his way to his laboratory to see if the experiment had been successful. Magic potions were bubbling and cooking away on the stoves and melting pots. The fires had cooled down under the crucible containing Monkey King. Only a few coals blinked among the gray ashes. Surely the smelting of Monkey King was complete.

Lao Tzu motioned for two servants to remove the lid. He blinked, and lo and behold, there was Monkey King rubbing his fiery eyes for all he was worth. Had he been asleep? Unbeliev-

able! Before Lao Tzu could think, Monkey King leaped out on the floor. Snatching some bright yellow powder from a pan, Monkey King threw it in their faces. It blinded them and made the most awful smell you can imagine.

"Sulphur dioxide," Lao Tzu said, rushing out of the laboratory.

"Rotten eggs," shrieked his servants close behind him, holding their noses.

In all the confusion of smelly gases in the air, no one saw which way Monkey King went. Not that it would have helped much, for by the time they came coughing and sputtering to their senses, Monkey King was far away.

Furious, Monkey King tore through Heaven like a knife slashing a painting, cutting everything in his path, smashing and destroying whomever and whatever he could. "I'll live forever and ever and ever," he shouted. Last seen he was heading toward the Hall of Magic Mists where he terrified the Kings of the Four Quarters. Monkey King couldn't stop bursting, breaking, smashing!

Such tumult! Everyone stayed away until, hopefully, some of his violence would be spent.

100

Finally the handsome Prince Natha and the thirty-six Thunder Deities cornered Monkey King by the jade fountain. Monkey King sensed that something was up and quickly changed himself into a monkey with six arms carrying six magic weapons. He spun around the fountain like a top until . . .

A voice as deep as the wind commanded him to halt.

Monkey stopped.

"I am the Lord Buddha, Supreme Ruler of the Universe," the voice said.

Monkey King wanted to reply, but the majesty of the Buddha forbade it. The Buddha commanded Prince Natha to lay down his arms and asked the Thunder Deities to retreat. Monkey King changed back into his old monkey self. As the Buddha approached, Monkey King caught sight of two disciples and a tall, beautiful woman carrying a willow sprig.

"That must be the Goddess of Mercy," Monkey King said to himself.

The Buddha addressed Monkey King. "The Jade Emperor tells me that you have been disturbing the realms of Heaven. Why are you

101

wasting your time? Were you not born of Heaven and Earth? Have you not been illumined?"

"It's true I was born of the union of Heaven and Earth. How did you know?"

The Buddha only smiled.

"I come from the Mountain of Flowers and Fruit by the Cave of the Water Curtain," cried Monkey King. "But I got tired of being king of the monkeys there. I wanted a crown of light like all those Immortals, so I went on a long journey until I found a holy man who had a crown of light, and he taught me many great secrets."

The compassion of the Buddha made Monkey King wish to tell all about himself. "I see," Buddha said, "and did he tell you to use them wisely?"

"Naturally. He taught me hundreds of tricks and transformations. I went to Heaven where I filled myself with peaches and elixers that make one live forever. Why, I am so full of essences that it's hard for me to stay on the ground. I need more elbowroom, larger spheres to move in and to rule. I have been the Great Sage, Equal of Heaven for long enough now. I am ready to challenge the Jade Emperor."

Buddha's disciples laughed nervously, and Kuan Yin smiled to herself. The Lord Buddha seated himself in the lotus position by the jade fountain.

"Do you know what a kalpa is?"

Monkey King shook his head.

"A kalpa is one hundred twenty-nine thousand years. The present Jade Emperor has been perfecting his wisdom for seventeen hundred and fifty kalpas. How many years is that?"

"How should I know?" Monkey King said brightly.

"Two hundred twenty-five million, seven hundred fifty thousand years. That is almost an immeasurable time. One might say that your life span has been rather short, Monkey. You are, after all, only a monkey spirit with large ideas, and you sometimes exceed yourself."

"But why should the Jade Emperor go on and on?" Monkey King persisted. "He was lucky that he was born so many thousands and thousands of years ago. What if I had been born before the Jade Emperor was? I could take

his place, and then there would be peace and quiet here."

Buddha's disciples looked at one another in horror. Monkey King had gone too far once again.

"I see. Just how do you propose to take over the many realms of Heaven?" asked the Buddha.

"Oh, I have lots of magic. I can change myself into any form I wish. I can streak like a shooting star through the sky as far as the Eastern Sea in one leap. I—"

"Well then," the Buddha said, "suppose we have a wager, you and I. Come down closer and I will tell you what it is."

Hopping along the edge of the jade fountain, Monkey stopped when he was almost sitting on the Buddha's knee. Kuan Yin drew closer and looked over the Buddha's shoulder. The Lord Buddha put forth his right hand.

"If you can somersault off the palm of my right hand, then you may take the place of the Jade Emperor. That is one part of my wager. If you succeed, then I will ask the Jade Emperor to come and live with me in the Western Paradise."

Monkey thought to himself. "I can jump anywhere I want. What a stupid fellow this Buddha is."

"But if you fail," the Lord Buddha said in a voice as deep as the wind, "then you must return at once to Earth and I will punish you for five hundred years. After that you may come again to seek me."

Monkey King could hardly wait to get started. He thought to himself, "It's at least one hundred and eight thousand leagues to the Eastern Sea, and I can jump there easily. But maybe he's trying to trick me because his hand is only a couple of inches across!" Then he said out loud. "You're certain this is on the level? I mean, suppose the Jade Emperor is not so anxious to leave his throne?"

"Oh, that can be arranged," the Lord Buddha assured Monkey King.

"Thank you," said Monkey King, hopping up on the palm of the Buddha's hand.

Monkey King made ready to jump. He concentrated hard and rose straight in the air. Confident of victory, he felt himself streaking through space as fast as ever. (Meanwhile the

Lord Buddha raised his Eye of Wisdom and looked down upon a tiny dot spinning along.)

Monkey King landed in front of five huge pink pillars. "This must be the end of the world. I've never seen anything like those before." He strutted about. Then he lifted his hind leg and relieved himself. "I'll be the Jade Emperor pretty soon. Hum dee-dee," he sang, skipping up and down and nodding to his imaginary subjects.

"Now I'll just write my name here, and then the people will know of my feat," he said to himself. So, plucking a hair from his side, he commanded it to change into a brush filled with ink. "THE NEW JADE EMPEROR WAS HERE," he wrote. He made his silver-white hair change back again. "Now I'll go back and tell that Buddha," he concluded. And he streaked back again through space.

"Where is my jade fan?" Monkey King asked upon his return. "You are looking at the new Jade Emperor."

"Foolish Monkey. You have lost the wager. The size of your world is smaller than you think."

"But I have proof that I flew to the end of the world."

"I am afraid that you have been strutting about the base of my middle finger. Look now and see what you wrote there," the Buddha said kindly.

Monkey King peered down at his flashy handwriting. "THE NEW JADE EMPEROR WAS HERE," it said.

He couldn't believe it. His astonishment grew like a balloon. Every time he gasped and let out a breath, it became larger. "You must have the whole world in your palm. I wrote in front of a pink pillar," he gasped, and his astonishment grew again. "How could it be your middle finger? I must go back and see."

Before Monkey King could leap, the Buddha turned his palm over, slapped him down, and pushed Monkey King out of Heaven. As Monkey King landed on earth, a very great weight pressed down on top of him. It was a five-peaked mountain which held him fast underneath. On the very top was the seal of the Buddha.

In his mercy, the Lord Buddha assigned several guards to watch over Monkey King.

The guards provided him with iron pills when he was hungry and molten bronze when he was thirsty.

"When the days of Monkey's penance are fulfilled, a guardian shall come down to release him," the Buddha commanded.

Epilogue

Who can say how long a day or an hour or a year or even a kalpa is? Or five hundred years? Sometimes an hour seems like a day. Sometimes a day becomes a year. If someone is waiting and waiting and waiting for a surprise, an hour may seem like a week. If someone is hoping for evil to pass away, a day may even become a year. But when one stands on a whole mountaintop of years, time flashes by.

Monkey King was under the Mountain of Five Elements for five hundred years. At the end of that time, when Kuan Yin and one of her disciples were on a special mission for the

Lord Buddha, they saw a shaft of yellow light streaming down from Heaven onto the mountain. Misty vapors rose about them as they approached in the air. When they landed on its top, they saw the seal of the Buddha.

"Isn't this the mountain under which that insolent Monkey is imprisoned?" Kuan Yin's disciple asked.

"It is indeed," said Kuan Yin smiling, "and it is time to have a talk with Monkey and see how he is."

"Who is up there?" a dry voice came from the little cave inside the mountain.

"I am Kuan Yin. Where are you?"

"Down here," Monkey King called up.

Kuan Yin and her disciple made their way down the craggy ledges toward the sound of Monkey King's thin voice. They found the guardian at the foot of the cliff, and he took them to the cave where Monkey King was prisoner. Monkey King's hair was even more silvery than Kuan Yin remembered, and his eyes, once hard and blazing, had grown softer and wiser. He peered out through a chink in one of the walls. "Ah, Kuan Yin, how glad I am to see you. No friend has come to see me in this place where the days and years are one. Pray tell me, where did you come from?"

"The Lord Buddha sent me to look for one who will go to India to obtain holy scriptures, and your mountain was on the way."

"May I come with you?"

"You used to say proud things," Kuan Yin said, shaking her head at Monkey King. "Your misdeeds in Heaven were numerous."

"Well, I did have a slight misunderstanding with the Lord Buddha, and he put me under this mountain. I've been here for five hundred years with nothing to do but think. I've decided to change. Please, won't you use your magic powers to rescue me? I promise that I won't get into trouble again."

Kuan Yin looked straight into Monkey King's soul. "Are you sure, Monkey?"

"Yes, I want to devote myself to good works and live the way a holy man once taught me."

Kuan Yin waved her willow branch like a fan. "Who was that, Monkey?"

"I promised not to tell," Monkey replied.

"It doesn't matter really—if you are clear about your new path. When I see the Jade Emperor and the Lord Buddha I shall ask them if they will release you," Kuan Yin said in her quiet voice.

Monkey King sneezed with delight. He knew that the gracious Kuan Yin would persuade them to let him go. At last his endless waiting would be over. When he came out, he'd return to his monkeys and be their king, possibly even a wise one.

Sally Hovey Wriggins was born and raised in Seattle, Washington. After receiving her Master's degree from Haverford College, she worked as a research analyst at the United Nations, and was a founder and the first chairperson of the Asian-American Forum in Washington, D.C. She is a member of the Bank Street Writer's Workshop and the Society of Women Geographers.

Ms. Wriggins and her family lived for several years in Asia and now make their home in New York, where her husband is Director of the Southern Asian Institute at Columbia University. *White Monkey King* is her first book for children.

Ronni Solbert, whose illustrations for *White Monkey King* are derived from traditional Chinese painting, is both a painter and sculptor. A graduate of Vassar College, she has illustrated over thirty children's books, including *A Few Flies and I*, *The Elephant Who Liked To Smash Small Cars*, and wrote as well as illustrated *Thirty-Two Feet of Insides*. Her work has appeared in museums throughout the country, and she has had a one-woman show at the Museum of Modern Art in New York. She lives in Randolph, Vermont.